The Traveller

Theresa Breslin

with illustrations by
Nelson Evergreen

Barrington Stoke

First published in 2013 in Great Britain by
Barrington Stoke Ltd
18 Walker Street, Edinburgh, EH3 7LP

www.barringtonstoke.co.uk

ISBN: 978-1-78112-198-6

Printed in China by Leo

This book is for Thom Mac Beatha

Chapter 1

Outside the inn, the wind was driving snow in from the north.

"It's on nights like this," the old man said, "that a stranger can lose his way."

"Easy for that to happen," the inn-keeper agreed, "when the night is so dark and snow covers all tracks."

"And sound too," the old man added. "Anything can stalk a man in the dark in the snow and wind. He doesn't hear the soft foot-fall behind him, or the breath of the hunter. Not until it's too late ..." He sighed.

"Do you think that was the way of it, then? All those years ago?" The question came from another man in the room.

"Who is to say?" the old man answered. He drank from his wine cup before he began again. "When the Traveller came here he was tall and proud and brave and ready to fight. At the time I thought that no one could defeat him. Not in fair combat, nor by cunning ..." He looked around at the listeners. "You would say that too if you had met him. But it was only I who saw him. It was only I who spoke to him that night. And it was I who let him go ..." He sighed again. "And he went to his death. I'm sure of it." He

paused as the wind shook the latches on the window shutters.

"Yes," he said. "It was on such a night as this. Heavy snow cloud was building in the Northlands, and the wind driving sleet before it, when my Traveller arrived."

The old man stopped speaking, then he tilted his wine cup and drained the last drops. He set it down with a thump. One of those beside him at the long table bent a finger at the inn-keeper. The inn-keeper rushed over with the wine jug.

The old man watched as his cup filled with the dark local wine. "Many times I've told this tale ..." he said. His voiced trailed away.

"It can bear another telling," came the reply.

Chapter 2

The old man nodded and spoke again.

"The sun had set in a blood red sky," he said. "There was a hard frost on tree and bush. And then snow came scurrying in on a cutting wind. Every living thing rushed to find shelter. And no more than an hour passed before a great snowstorm raged down into the valley."

He looked at the door. Outside the gale howled and tore at the roof tiles.

"Like tonight," the old man said. He lowered his voice to a whisper. "Mark my words well, now. It was just like this very night."

The folk in the inn drew closer together as the old man went on. "I was sitting where I am now," he said. "When the storm was at its wildest, the inn door crashed open and a man stood in the doorway."

The old man paused for breath and lifted his cup to his lips. Just as he wiped his mouth, the door of the inn flew open and slammed back as the wind took it.

"Mercy, save us!" the old man gasped in alarm. He made the sign to ward off evil.

"A bad omen," someone remarked.

"Nonsense!" said the inn-keeper. "'Tis only another traveller!" He hurried over to the young man who stood in the doorway.

"Come up to the fire, boy, and warm yourself." He took the stranger by the arm to help him in.

Chapter 3

The boy at the door stamped the snow from his boots and shook out the folds of his cloak. Then he looked about him.

"Here, by the chimney," the inn-keeper said.

The boy walked to the fireplace. He kept the hood of his cloak up as he sat down and stretched his long legs before the flames.

The old man who was telling the story screwed up his eyes and peered at the boy. He shook his head. "Another traveller?" he muttered. "Strange ..."

"Aye, and it was strange that night, fifteen years ago, by all accounts," said one of the company, who was keen to hear the rest of the old man's tale.

The old man picked up his wine and his story.

"We don't much take to strangers in these parts," he said. "Can't be doing with nosy folk asking questions. The troubles we have are troubles enough."

"Aye." A murmur of agreement went round the table. "And there's no way to rid ourselves of those troubles."

Under the hood of his cloak the boy by the fire turned his head to listen.

"No, we don't take to strangers," the old man said, "but this Traveller who stood in our inn door that night was different. We could tell he was weary for he swayed on his feet. I went to help him. I was inn-keeper here then, and I knew my duty. He was a tall man, with eyes of sharp blue, deep-set in a bearded face. There was a grim purpose in his manner. And he was proud too, for he tried to shake off my helping hand, and at first refused my offer of a warm drink.

'I must go on,' the Traveller said. 'I saw your light, and only stopped to ask the way.'

I poured him some warm wine. 'From where have you come?' I asked him.

'South,' he said.

I laughed. 'Then South is where you must return,' I said. 'There is no way on from here. This inn is named 'Road End' for a reason. East is the sea, with only a huddle of houses by the shore. To the

North the mountain passes are blocked until late Spring.'

As I finished speaking the Traveller grasped my arm. 'And what lies West?' he demanded.

I dropped my eyes. Such awful stories to tell, if I were to give him a true answer to his question.

'Nothing but ill lies to the West,' I told him."

"Aye, that is the truth," one of the old man's cronies broke in. "And so it is today, still."

The inn-keeper paused in the act of filling the cups, and spat on the floor. "A curse on the Lord of Aleslan, murderer and widow-maker."

Chapter 4

The boy by the fire drew his hood closer.

"It was as bad then as now," the old man said. "Taxes that tenants could not afford. Widows driven from their miserable hovels. Roofs set on fire over

the heads of the old who could not find the means to pay their rent."

"And you told the Traveller all of this?" The inn-keeper asked the question to keep the story and the wine flowing.

"He wanted to know every detail," the old man said. "And the more he heard, the angrier he grew, until I feared that he might draw the silver sword that hung at his belt and use it on me."

The old man broke off and looked over to the fire, where the boy sat in the shadow of the great chimney. He shook his head and murmured the word, "strange ..." again, half to himself. Then he went on with his story.

"I told the Traveller of the first Lord Aleslan. How he had been full of wisdom, but also full of age, and that he had died some years before. I let him know how much we had loved our noble Lord who protected us and made sure that his people were fed and cared for.

Then I told him of Aleslan's son, banished by his father for his foul deeds and evil ways. He was a man we thought never to see again. But of course he returned on his father's death to become the new Lord Aleslan.

I explained to the Traveller how we hoped that the son had changed and given up his wicked ways, for he had brought home a young wife. She was beautiful and good and gave food and money to the poor. We thought he would follow her example and be kind to us. But no! He took his father's lands and tenants under his cruel command. His wife was a fragile flower, and he allowed her no friends, so she soon began to pine. I told the Traveller how the new Lord Aleslan kept her prisoner in his Castle. And after she had given him the son he craved, she became ill, and he would not summon the doctor, but left her to die."

The old man brushed tears from his eyes.

"When I told the Traveller that the girl had passed on he became as one mad. He

grabbed my shoulders and shook me till my teeth rattled.

'She is dead?' he cried. 'You are sure of this?'

I could only nod. And he fell silent and was still for a long moment. Then he gave a start. 'And what of the child?' he asked.

'Healthy and well ... at least in body,' I said. 'But now he is left in the care of that wicked man, it will not be long before poison flows in his veins too.'

My Traveller put his hand to his sword. 'Then it is even more important now that I go at once to the Castle of Aleslan,' he said.

And he went to the inn door and opened it. Outside, the shroud of the night was bleak and bitter."

The old man shook his head.

"I tried to stop him leaving. 'Don't go,' I begged him. 'Hold off until dawn. Whatever business you have with the Lord Aleslan can wait until morning.'

But my Traveller looked back at me.

'The business I have to do,' he said, 'is best done in the dark.'"

Chapter 5

The old man's voice was very low as he finished his tale. "The Traveller went out into the night, and we never saw him again."

"Nor heard any word of him?"

The question came from the boy by the fire.

The old man jumped at the sound of his voice. "We heard that he did enter the Castle of Aleslan," he replied. "I had hoped that the Traveller was a hero who would free us. That he would slay our evil Lord with his silver sword. He did not do so. Instead ... he stole the child."

"Ah!" There was a sharp breath from the boy. "So it *is* true," he said softly. He

raised his voice to ask, "Did Lord Aleslan try to follow your Traveller?"

"Lord Aleslan hunted my Traveller day and night in every direction, but he was never found. There was not a track to follow anywhere. They say he must have tried to find a way through the snowy mountains. If he did that, then he is sure to have perished." The old man shook his head. "All we know is that things have gone from bad to worse. Starving children caught snaring rabbits in his woods lie rotting in the prison of Lord Aleslan's Castle."

"Yet it was wrong to take the child as revenge," said one of the listeners. "That poor babe died because the Traveller loved its mother, and lost her to Aleslan."

"No." The boy by the fire spoke again. "What your Traveller did was not for revenge. He carried the child to safety through the Northern passes for love, it is true. But it was the love that a brother bears his sister. For his sister had sent word to him to rescue her from her madman husband, and he came as fast as he could. Alas, it was too late ... too late for her, but ..."

The boy got to his feet and threw back the hood of his cloak. "But not for me," he said.

And for the first time the folk in the inn saw the face of the boy who had come to seek shelter from the storm. He stood tall, with a proud look and deep set blue eyes.

Chapter 6

"When I was growing up," said the boy, "I often wondered who my mother and father were. My uncle never told me the true story of how I came to be brought up in his home. He let me believe that both my parents died when I was a baby, and that, since my mother was his sister, it was his place to look after me. I know now that it was he who came to Castle Aleslan and rescued me. It was he who made the daring trip through the mountains with me slung across his back."

The old man gave a cry and rose from his seat. "You are the stolen child!" he gasped.

"I am," the boy replied. "In all the years he raised me, my uncle did not break his silence about my birth. But when he died I found my mother's letters to him, and I

knew that I must come here to seek the truth."

"The truth is the story I have told this night," said the old man.

"After this night is over you will have another story to tell," the boy told him. He cast his cloak back from his shoulders so that they could all see the silver sword hanging from his belt.

"I go from my past to my future," he said. "And I promise you that, by morning, there will be no child kept prisoner in the Castle of Aleslan."

"Don't go!" The old man reached out his arms. "You will disappear as my Traveller did and never be heard of again"

"Oh, you will hear, and see, what I am about to do," the boy said. His face was grim as he bent down and took a long stick of burning wood from the fire. Then he walked across the room and opened the door of the inn.

"Stop him!" the old man shouted. "If you try to free the prisoners Lord Aleslan will kill you. A man with a heart as hard as his would not think twice before he killed his own son. If you must go, at least wait till dawn."

The boy turned in the door and smiled. "The business I have to do," he said, "is best done in the dark."

Chapter 7

Outside the inn, the wind was driving snow in from the north.

"It's on nights like this," the old man said, "that a stranger can lose his way."

"Easy for that to happen," the inn-
keeper agreed, "when the night is so dark
and snow covers all tracks."

"Yes," the old man went on. "It was on
such a night as this ... Heavy snow cloud
was building in the Northlands, and the
wind driving sleet before it, when our
Traveller arrived."

The old man stopped speaking, then
he tilted his wine cup and drained the last
drops. He set it down with a thump. One
of those beside him at the long table bent

a finger at the inn-keeper. The inn-keeper rushed over with the wine jug.

The old man watched as his cup filled with the dark local wine. "Many times in this inn I've told tales of Travellers," he said, "but this is the best tale of all."

"What makes it the best tale of all?" asked someone in the room.

"It is the best because it is the tale of how a wicked lord was beheaded with a silver sword. Of how prisoners were freed

from deep dungeons. Of how one dark night Aleslan Castle was set on fire so that everyone in the village could see it burn. Of how we heard the voices of our children again and knew that our days of slavery were over."

"And the Traveller who came to the inn that night?" one of the listeners asked.

"Let us drink a toast to him." The old man raised his wine cup. "For that Traveller became the good Lord Aleslan who rules our land today."

*Also by **Theresa Breslin**...*

Prisoner in Alcatraz

It is your right to have: food,
clothing, shelter and medical attention.
Anything else you get is a privilege.

Marty is doing life in the hardest prison in
America. No one gets out of Alcatraz. But now
there's a new escape plan. Can Marty break out
of Alcatraz – or will life mean life?

Alligator

"Pssst... Wanna buy an alligator?"

Jono's mum is going to kill him.
He didn't mean to buy an alligator.
It just sort of happened.

Laugh-out-loud comedy.

Also available as a play!

www.barringtonstoke.co.uk

More *great reads* to try...

Jon for Short
MALORIE BLACKMAN

As the blade flashed down in the dim light, it seemed to wink, wink, wink...

Jon is in hospital. He can't move.

The doctors have taken his arms and he is sure his legs are next.

Will Jon ever escape?

Awesome
PETE JOHNSON

The girls at school are convinced that shy new boy Ben is the star of the hit show *Awesome*.

Surely there can be no harm in Ben playing along...?

Respect!
MICHAELA MORGAN

When their mum and dad die, Tully and his brother are sent to a Children's Home.

Life is hard. But Tully has an amazing talent that will win him a place in history.

Based on a true story.

Mutant
THERESA BRESLIN

Someone is trying to destroy the data and steal the work in the clone unit. But who is it and why are they doing it?

Anything could happen if the research gets into the wrong hands. So who can Brad trust?

www.barringtonstoke.co.uk